These Are My
Christmas Wishes
for You

Library of Congress Catalog Card Number: 96-32025
ISBN: 0-88396-439-2

Acknowledgments:
I would like to thank the wonderful people at Blue Mountain Arts for their
creative talents and continued support, and I would like to dedicate this book to
the memory of my brother, Roger William Pagels.

⌂ design on book cover is registered in
U.S. Patent and Trademark Office.

Manufactured in the United States of America
First Printing: August, 1996

Library of Congress Cataloging-in-Publication Data
Pagels, Douglas.
    These are my Christmas wishes for you : a special holiday
collection / by Douglas Pagels.
      p.   cm.
    ISBN 0-88396-439-2 (softcover : alk. paper)
    1. Christmas—Miscellanea.   I. Title.
BV45.P33   1996
242'.33—dc20   96-32025
                                               CIP

This book is printed on fine quality, laid embossed, 80 lb. paper. This paper has been
specially produced to be acid free (neutral pH) and contains no groundwood or
unbleached pulp. It conforms with all of the requirements of the American National
Standards Institute, Inc., so as to ensure that this book will last and be enjoyed by
future generations.

Blue Mountain Press ®

P.O. Box 4549, Boulder, Colorado 80306

These Are My
Christmas Wishes
for You

A special holiday collection

by Douglas Pagels

Happy Holidays!

May You Always Have an
ANGEL
by Your Side

May you always have an angel by your side ❧ Watching out for you in all the things you do ❧ Reminding you to keep believing in brighter days ❧ Finding ways for your wishes and dreams to take you to beautiful places ❧ Giving you hope that is as certain as the sun ❧ Giving you the strength of serenity as your guide ❧ May you always have love and comfort and courage ❧ And may you always have an angel by your side...

May you always have an angel by your side ❧
Someone there to catch you if you fall ❧
Encouraging your dreams ❧ Inspiring your
happiness ❧ Holding your hand and helping
you through it all ❧

In all of our days, our lives are always changing ❧
Tears come along as well as smiles ❧ Along the roads
you travel, may the miles be a thousand times more
lovely than lonely ❧ May they give you gifts that
never, ever end: someone wonderful to love and a dear
friend in whom you can confide ❧ May you have
rainbows after every storm ❧ May you have hopes to
keep you warm ❧

And may you always have an angel by your side ❧

May you hold on to your dreams and never let them go. Show the rest of the world what I already know: how wonderful you are!

Wish on a star that shines in your sky. Continue to look on the bright side.

I want you to always be yourself, because you are filled with special qualities that have brought you this far, and that will always see you through.

Keep your spirits up. Make your heart happy, and let it reflect on everything you do!

I want you to know
that one of the most
important things
in this world
is your presence in it.

I want the things you do
to turn into the nicest memories
any person could ever ask for.

I Wish for You These
24 Things to Always Remember...
and One Thing to Never Forget

Your presence is a present to the world.
You're unique and one of a kind.
Your life can be what you want it to be.
Take the days just one at a time.

Count your blessings, not your troubles.
You'll make it through whatever comes along.
Within you are so many answers.
Understand, have courage, be strong.

Don't put limits on yourself.
So many dreams are waiting to be realized.
Decisions are too important to leave to chance.
Reach for your peak, your goal, your prize.

Nothing wastes more energy than worrying.
The longer one carries a problem,
   the heavier it gets.
Don't take things too seriously.
Live a life of serenity, not a life of regrets.

Remember that a little love goes a long way.
Remember that a lot... goes forever.
Remember that friendship is a wise investment.
Life's treasures are people... together.

Realize that it's never too late.
Do ordinary things in an extraordinary way.
Have health and hope and happiness.
Take the time to wish upon a star.

And don't ever forget...
   for even a day... how very special you are.

I want you to think
about getting rich:

Friendships are priceless,
time is invaluable,
health is wealth,
and love is a treasure.

May you always hold on
to the secret of making
your good times better
and your hard times a little
easier to handle.

I want you to have millions
of moments when you find
satisfaction in the things
you do so wonderfully.

And I wish I could find a way
to tell you — in untold ways —
how important you are to me.

May you always remember
that there are so many admirable,
one-of-a-kind things about you.
And may you never forget
that if you can search within and
find a smile… that smile will
always be a reflection of the way
people, like me, feel about you.

I want you to promise me this:

Promise me you'll always remember
what a worthy person you are ❧
Promise me you'll hold on to your
hopes and reach out for your stars ❧
Promise me you'll "remember when"
and you'll always "look forward to…"
❧ Promise me you'll do the things you
always wanted to do ❧ Promise me
you'll live with happiness over the
years and over the miles ❧ And promise
me that when you think of me, it will
always be with a smile.

I wish you promises that lie
before you: of brighter days,
of worthwhile directions to go in,
and of golden opportunities
that open wide their doors.
I wish for every happiness in
life to be yours.

I wish you contentment: the
sweet, quiet, inner kind that
comes around and never goes away.

I wish you the closeness of people who can guide you, inspire you, comfort you, and light up your life with laughter. I want your life to overlap with the lives of those who understand your moods, who nurture your needs, and who lovingly know just what you're after.

As your mailbox fills up with holiday cards and letters coming from every direction under the sun, may you smile to realize how easily distances are shortened between the hearts of caring people.

Time does pass, and we do change and grow, but growing apart is not an option for those who know that love lives in a place where time matters not, and that friendship inhabits a space where affectionate wishes turn into magical bridges which can easily span thousands of miles. A simple card, a stamp, and a few words written with a loving pen can keep two friends close forever.

May you have feelings that are
shared from heart to heart,
simple pleasures amidst this
complex world, and visionary
goals that are within your grasp.

I want you to keep planting the
seeds of your dreams... because if
you keep believing in them,
they'll keep trying their best
to blossom for you.

I want you to remember that
time can't take away anything
that has already been given:
Your treasures from days gone by
are treasures still, and your most
precious memories will always be.

We learn, as we go along, that life
is not one big, beautiful jewel we
can hold — or lose — in our hands.
Each one of us is an hourglass. And
in the course of our lives, we get to
keep all the diamonds that come
our way among the passing sands.

In the story of your life, may you write the very best book you can. Have pages on understanding and tales of overcoming hardships. Fill your story with romance, adventure, poetry, and laughter. Make each chapter reflect time well spent.

I wish you a joyous spirit and a sensitive soul, and I want those qualities to be appreciated to their fullest by all those who know you.

I will always hope that the people who share your life are special, insightful people who realize how lucky they are to be in the presence of a present like you.

I want you to know that you may
be down-to-earth, but you feel
a lot like a gift from above.

May you understand that there are
so many special dimensions to your
life, and one of the ones you
should be most proud of... is that
you do the things you do with love.

I want you to chase after your highest hopes and hold on tight ❧ Live according to your innermost plan ❧ Imagine things you've always wanted to come true ❧ Discover their truths inside of you ❧ Make tomorrow happier by traveling there in ways that really matter ❧ And don't ever forget that, eventually, dream-chasers become dream-catchers.

I want you to imagine what you can accomplish — if you accomplish even half of what you can imagine.

I want you, whenever you're wondering what path to take, to do some soul-searching about how you want things to be, and then a lot of goal-reaching to make them that way.

I want you to know that you are capable of working miracles of your own making.

May you refrain from putting
any limits on yourself.
Amaze yourself with what you
discover you can do.

I want everything
to work out for you
just the way
you want it to.

May you know how capable
you are of touching the lives
of others. In a way that is
appreciated beyond words,
you have given more meaning
to my days than you will ever
know, and you have given me
gifts that I will take with me
for the rest of my life...
everywhere I go.

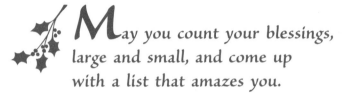

May you count your blessings,
large and small, and come up
with a list that amazes you.

May you have a quiet place
in your heart where your
nicest thoughts all meet
for serenity and safekeeping.

May you have an inner vision
that never lets you lose sight of the
things that are truly important.

May you have a wonderful
camaraderie with the people
you trust enough to share your
shortcomings, your highest hopes,
your most serious thoughts, and
your silliest jokes.

May you have the kind of people
in your world who see the horizon
from your point of view, and who
sometimes help you to see more
clearly.

I want you to receive, from these
people, honesty and trust enfolded
with love.

May you realize what a valuable
gift you give when you truly
give of yourself.

I want you to remember that if you can dream it, you can probably make it come true. Build creative bridges to get where you're going. Appreciate all the special qualities within you.

Don't let worries get in the way of recognizing how great things can be. Always keep moving ahead. Live to the fullest and make each day count. Don't let the important things go unsaid.

Don't just have minutes in the day; have moments in time. Balance out any bad with the good you can provide. Know that you are capable of amazing results. Discover new strengths inside.

May you add a meaningful page to the diary of each new day. Do things that lift your spirits and help you rise above. Walk along the pathways that lead to more happiness. And give your tomorrows what your yesterdays have only seen a glimpse of.

I wish you wondrous things that can't be tied up in ribbons and bows. I wish you thoughts that take you to magnificent places. I wish you togetherness and abundant happiness. I wish you soaring hopes for the days ahead and profound joys for the year that has been.

And I wish you quiet times all to yourself, when the grace of all that is good in your life is sweetly celebrated within.

May you embrace the new times ahead and confront, courageously, whatever trials they may hold.

I wish you a gentle reminder that having a sense of humor helps you to survive, and that it pays such nice dividends. When everything seems to go wrong — your outlook can go a long way to help you handle anything that can arrive.

I wish you joy and laughter — and the simple pleasure of being alive.

May you discover some
holiday ways of making
the children happy and —
remembering that kids
come in all sizes and that
children come in all ages —
may one of those happy
faces be yours.

I wish you the comfort of a true companion: a hand that is always holding yours, no matter where you are, no matter how close or far apart you may be.

May you have the type of friendship that is a treasure and the kind of love that is beautiful forever.

May you create lasting
changes in your life and in the
way you want tomorrow to be.

I want you to have choices to
make and challenges to meet
that will give you the chance
to really be all that you are
capable of becoming.

May you remember that
though the roads we take can
sometimes be difficult,
those are often the ones that
lead to the most beautiful views.

I wish you patience, when
patience is exactly what
the situation calls for.

I want you to always have the
ability to rise above misfortune
and the reminder that help is
always reaching out, always close,
always there anytime you need it.

When feelings overflow and tears
need to fall, I want you to have
someone to help you through it all.

I wish you the good things in life, and I pray that some of those things will be your happiness and good health, close friends, a loving family, and all that success means to you. And remember that those good things also include: the knowledge of all that you are to me, the gratitude of others when you are near, and the quiet contentment of a gently smiling face... returning your smile in the mirror.

I want you to be truly happy. To discover some more sweetness within the days. To be given some more serenity. To search out more rainbows. To find some more time that is yours to spend as wisely and as wonderfully as you can.

I want you to listen to your heart. To hear what any frustrations have to say and to find a better way. To know what brings you smiles — the very best kind — the "this is what it's all about" kind.

I want you to reach out to the people you are close to and to find yourself in the places that mean the most to you.

I want you to build bridges that
will take you to brighter tomorrows.
To find solace in the simpler things.
To hold on to the joy of your moments,
the love, the laughter, the inner smiles,
and the dreams in which you believe.

I want you to remember that the
happiness you create today will remain
forever in your memories. I want you
to live by your own light and shine by
your own star. I want you to do what
you always wanted to do with your life.

I want you to envision
the gift that you are.

May a gently falling snow nestle against the windows of your dreams on Christmas Eve, and may your silent night be warmed by the thought that the gifts of peace and goodwill may someday come to us all. May you imagine a time when anyone having difficult days will be able to see their way through, and may the whole world wake up on Christmas morning to discover... that some dreams really do come true.

May you have a strong belief
in yourself — one that will
always make a difference
in your days.

May you never feel
threatened by the future
or bothered by the past.

May you feel that each
new day is a gift
you have been given.
May you open that gift
with childlike anticipation
and close the door at the
end of each day with a
prayerful appreciation.

I wish you sweet dreams. I want you to have times when you feel like singing and dancing and laughing out loud.

I want you to learn so much from the world around you; from the words you read, the places you go, the faces you see. Even during the course of your daily tasks, I want you to discover a vantage point that provides you with a rewarding perspective. I want you to make the commonplace a wondrous place to be.

I want this season to light
up your life and live on in
your heart long after
Christmas has departed.

I want every month,
as it comes your way, to stay
close to your heart and for
each week to have something
about it that makes it seem
like your favorite.

I want to wish you a world
where every single day
has a little bit
        of Christmas
            in it.

I wish I could find a way
to let you know how much
nicer life is… with you here.

I want you to pat yourself
on the back and be glad
that you leave so many
smiles on people's faces.

I want you to have as much
happiness as tomorrow can
promise to anyone.

I would like you to know, today and always, that there aren't many people in this whole wide world who even begin to compare with you.

*A*nd now, as this book comes to a close,
there are two special things
I want you to remember...

I hope you have a wonderful,
happy holiday filled with love
and the light of friendship's glow.

And I hope
the year ahead
will take you
everywhere your wishes
have always wanted to go!